A Beginning-to-Read Book

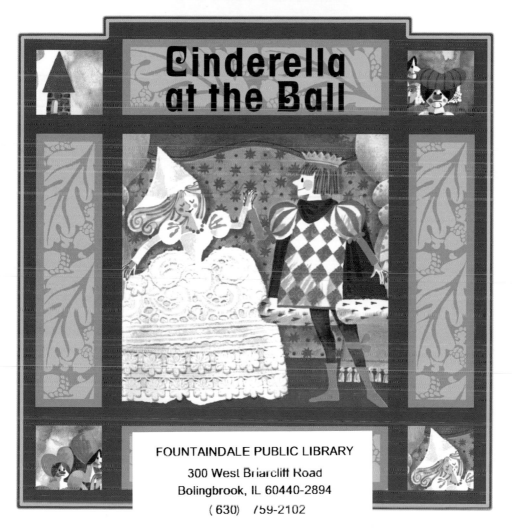

Cinderella at the Ball

by Margaret Hillert

Illustrated by Janet LaSalle

NORWOODHOUSE PRESS

DEAR CAREGIVER,

The *Beginning-to-Read* series is a carefully written collection of classic readers you may remember from your own childhood. Each book features text comprised of common sight words to provide your child ample practice reading the words that appear most frequently in written text. The many additional details in the pictures enhance the story and offer the opportunity for you to help your child expand oral language and develop comprehension.

Begin by reading the story to your child, followed by letting him or her read familiar words and soon your child will be able to read the story independently. At each step of the way, be sure to praise your reader's efforts to build his or her confidence as an independent reader. Discuss the pictures and encourage your child to make connections between the story and his or her own life. At the end of the story, you will find reading activities and a word list that will help your child practice and strengthen beginning reading skills.

Above all, the most important part of the reading experience is to have fun and enjoy it!

Shannon Cannon

Shannon Cannon,
Literacy Consultant

Norwood House Press • P.O. Box 316598 • Chicago, Illinois 60631
For more information about Norwood House Press please visit our website at *www.norwoodhousepress.com* or call 866-565-2900.

LIBRARY OF CONGRESS CATALOGING-IN-PUBLICATION DATA
 Hillert, Margaret.
  Cinderella at the ball / by Margaret Hillert; illustrated by Janet LaSalle. — Rev. and expanded library ed.
   p. cm. — (Beginning-to-read book)
  Summary: Retells the story of Cinderella going to the ball aided by her fairy godmother. Includes reading activities.
  ISBN-13: 978-1-59953-046-8 (library binding : alk. paper)
  ISBN-10: 1-59953-046-5 (library binding : alk. paper)
  [1. Fairy tales. 2. Folklore.] I. LaSalle, Janet, ill. II. Title. III. Series: Hillert, Margaret. Beginning to read series. Fairy tales and folklore.
  PZ8.H5425 Ci
  398.2—dc22
  [E]   2006007890

Come to the ball!
Come to the ball!

Oh, Mother, Mother.
We can go to the ball.
We two can go.
A ball is fun.

Come here, you.
Run, run, run.
You can help.
We want you to help.

Look here, Mother.
Here we go.
Away, away.

I want to come, too.
A ball is fun.

You!
You go to the ball!
Oh, not you.
You look funny.
And you can not come.

9

I can not go.
I look funny.
Oh my, oh my.

Look up, little one.
Look up and see me.
I can help you.
You can go, too.

See here.
I can make something for you.
One, two, three!
Here it is.

And look here.
Here is something big and orange.
You can go to the ball in it.

Here it is.
It is for you.
Go in, go in.

Look, look.
One little one.
Two little ones.
Three little ones.

See here.
One big one.
Two big ones.
Three big ones.

Away you go.
Away, little one.
Away to the ball.
A ball is fun.

Here I go.
Up, up, up.
Up to the ball.

Oh my, oh my.
It is fun here.
Fun for you and me.

Oh, look.
Oh, oh, oh.
Here I go.
Run, run, run.

Where is the little one?
Find the little one for me.
Go and look.
Go, go.

Where is the little one?
Come here.
Come here.
We want to find you.

Not you.
Not you.
It is not you.
Go away.
Go away.

27

Here you are, little one.
I like you.
Come with me to my house.

The following activities support the findings of the National Reading Panel that determined the most effective components for reading instruction are: Phonemic Awareness, Phonics, Vocabulary, Fluency, and Text Comprehension.

Phonemic Awareness: The soft c sound

Oddity Task: Say the soft **c** sound (as in Cinderella) for your child. Ask your child to say the word that has the soft **c** sound in the following word groups:

city, car, cap	can, center, candy	care, camp, circle
cell, call, cat	rack, rock, race	coin, cent, cat

Phonics: The letters c, e, and i

1. Demonstrate how to form the letters **c**, **e**, and **i** for your child.
2. Have your child practice writing **c**, **e**, and **i** at least three times each.
3. Point to the word Cinderella on the front cover. Explain to your child that when **c** is followed by the letters **i** or **e**, it sounds like /**s**/.
4. Write the following words on separate pieces of paper. Say each word and ask your child to tell you if the word has a soft **c** or hard **c** sound. If it has a soft **c** sound, ask your child to circle the letter that makes the **c** soft:

cent	cat	cricket	circle	cell
rock	race	city	cart	center

5. Ask your child to read each completed word, provide help sounding them out as needed.

Vocabulary: Homophones

1. Explain to your child that sometimes we combine two words that can sound alike and are sometimes spelled the same way but mean different things. These kinds of words are called homophones.

2. Point to the word Ball on the front cover. Ask your child what the word means. If your child doesn't know explain that it is a fancy party with dancing. Ask your child to tell you about a different meaning for ball.

3. Write the following words on separate pieces of paper:

night	rap	pane	toe	hare	sail	mail
meet	brake	I	red	tale	deer	eight
knight	wrap	pain	tow	hair	sale	male
meat	break	eye	read	tail	dear	ate

4. Read each word to your child.

5. Mix up the words and ask your child to match the homophone pairs.

6. Ask your child to tell you what each word means. If your child doesn't know, discuss the different meanings for each homophone pair and point to the word to help your child recognize the right spelling.

Fluency: Shared Reading

1. Reread the story to your child at least two more times while your child tracks the print by running a finger under the words as they are read. Ask your child to read the words he or she knows with you.

2. Reread the story taking turns, alternating readers between sentences or pages.

Text Comprehension: Discussion Time

1. Ask your child to retell the sequence of events in the story.

2. To check comprehension, ask your child the following questions:

- Why didn't the sisters want Cinderella to go to the ball?
- How did the fairy godmother help Cinderella?
- What did she turn the mice in to?
- How did the prince find Cinderella?
- Which parts of this story could really happen?
- Which parts of this story could not really happen?
- What lesson do you think the sisters learned?

Cinderella at the Ball uses the 44 words listed below.

This list can be used to practice reading the words that appear in the text. You may wish to write the words on index cards and use them to help your child build automatic word recognition. Regular practice with these words will enhance your child's fluency in reading connected text.

a	help	not	up
and	here		
are	house	oh	want
away		one(s)	we
	I	orange	where
ball	in		with
big	is	run	
	it		you
can		see	
come	little	something	
	look		
find		the	
for	make	three	
fun	me	to	
funny	mother	too	
	my	two	
go			

ABOUT THE AUTHOR Margaret Hillert has written over 80 books for children who are just learning to read. Her books have been translated into many different languages and over a million children throughout the world have read her books. She first started writing poetry as a child and has continued to write for children and adults throughout her life. A first grade teacher for 34 years, Margaret is now retired from teaching and lives in Michigan where she likes to write, take walks in the morning, and care for her three cats.

Photograph by Glenna Washburn

ABOUT THE ADVISER Shannon Cannon contributed the activities pages that appear in this book. Shannon serves as a literacy consultant and provides staff development to help improve reading instruction. She is a frequent presenter at educational conferences and workshops. Prior to this she worked as an elementary school teacher and as president of a curriculum publishing company.